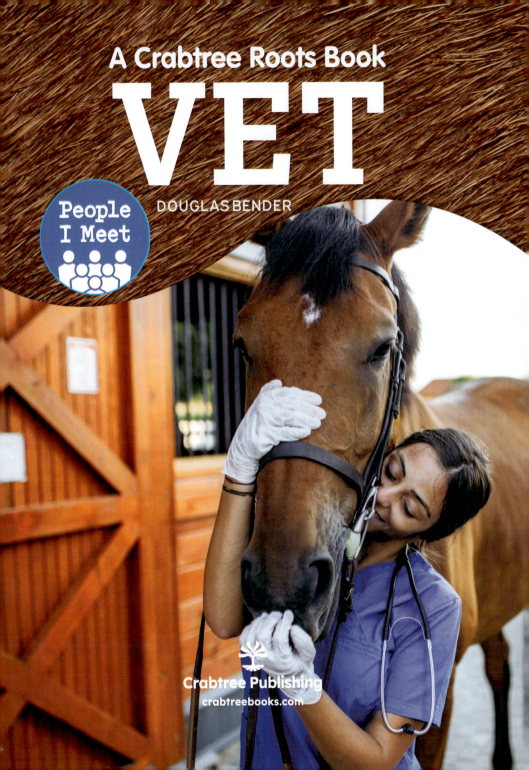

School-to-Home Support for Caregivers and Teachers

This book helps children grow by letting them practice reading. Here are a few guiding questions to help the reader with building his or her comprehension skills. Possible answers appear here in red.

Before Reading:

- What do I think this book is about?
  - *This book is about vets.*
  - *This book is about what a vet does at work.*
- What do I want to learn about this topic?
  - *I want to learn where a vet works.*
  - *I want to learn what a vet does.*

During Reading:

- I wonder why...
  - *I wonder why people become vets.*
  - *I wonder why vets give animals shots.*
- What have I learned so far?
  - *I have learned that some vets help small animals.*
  - *I have learned that vets give animals medicine.*

After Reading:

- What details did I learn about this topic?
  - *I have learned that not all vets know how to help all animals.*
  - *I have learned that animals need shots to be healthy.*
- Read the book again and look for the vocabulary words.
  - *I see the word **medicine** on page 8 and the word **shot** on page 10. The other vocabulary words are found on page 14.*

This is a **vet**.

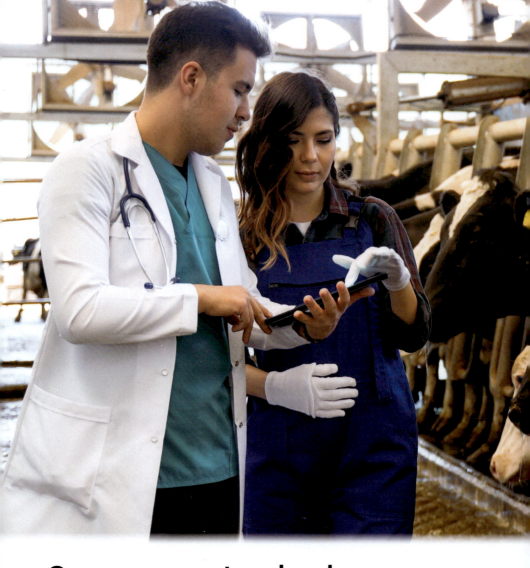

Some vets help big **animals**.

Some vets help small animals.

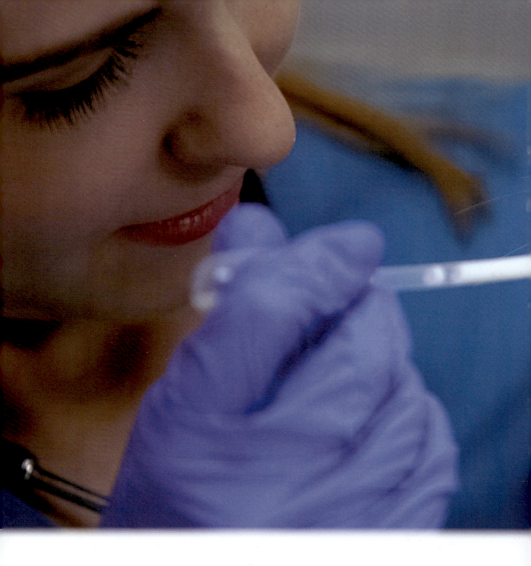

A vet gives an animal **medicine**.

A vet gives an animal a **shot**.

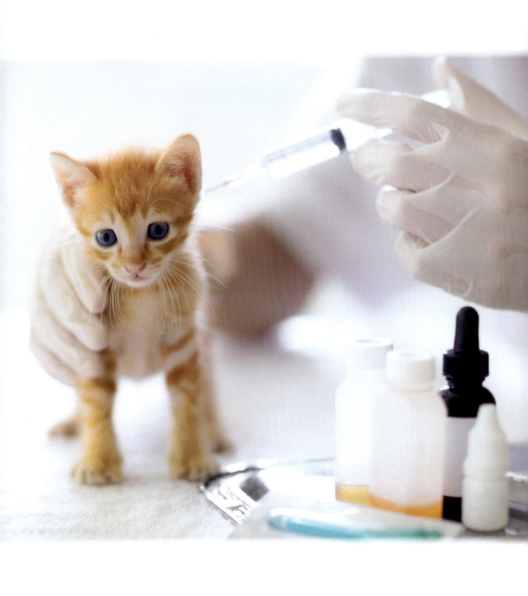

Do you know a vet?

Word List

Sight Words

a	is	you
an	some	
do	this	

Words to Know

animals

medicine

shot

vet

32 Words

This is a **vet**.

Some vets help big **animals**.

Some vets help small animals.

A vet gives an animal **medicine**.

A vet gives an animal a **shot**.

Do you know a vet?

People I Meet
VET

Photographs:
Shutterstock: The_Molostock: cover; hedgehog94: p. 1; santypan: p.3, 13, 14; BBSTUDIOPHOTO: p. 4-5, 14; JuiceFair: p. 6; Motortian Films: p. 8-9; FamVeld: p. 11

Crabtree Publishing

crabtreebooks.com   800-387-7650
Copyright © 2022 Crabtree Publishing

All rights reserved. No part of this publication may be reproduced, stored in a retrieval system or be transmitted in any form or by any means, electronic, mechanical, photocopying, recording, or otherwise, without the prior written permission of Crabtree Publishing Company. In Canada: We acknowledge the financial support of the Government of Canada through the Canada Book Fund for our publishing activities.

Written by: Douglas Bender
Designed by: Rhea Wallace
Series Development: James Earley
Proofreader: Ellen Rodger
Educational Consultant: Marie Lemke M.Ed.

Published in Canada
Crabtree Publishing
616 Welland Avenue
St. Catharines, Ontario
L2M 5V6

Published in the United States
Crabtree Publishing
347 Fifth Avenue
Suite 1402-145
New York, NY 10016

Hardcover	978-1-4271-4117-0
Paperback	978-1-4271-4123-1
Ebook (pdf)	978-1-4271-3346-5
Epub	978-1-4271-3406-6
Read-along	978-1-4271-4129-3
Audio book	978-1-4271-3921-4

Printed in the U.S.A./112023/PP20230920

Library and Archives Canada Cataloguing in Publication

Title: Vet / Douglas Bender.
Names: Bender, Douglas, 1992- author.
Description: Series statement: People I meet | "A Crabtree roots book".
Identifiers: Canadiana (print) 20210178655 | Canadiana (ebook) 20210178663 | ISBN 9781427141170 (hardcover) | ISBN 9781427141231 (softcover) | ISBN 9781427133465 (HTML) | ISBN 9781427134066 (EPUB) | ISBN 9781427141293 (read-along ebook)
Subjects: LCSH: Veterinarians—Juvenile literature.
Classification: LCC SF756 .B46 2022 | DDC j636.089/069—dc23

Library of Congress Cataloging-in-Publication Data

Names: Bender, Douglas, 1992- author.
Title: Vet / Douglas Bender.
Description: New York : Crabtree Publishing, 2022. | Series: People I meet - A Crabtree Roots book | Includes index.
Identifiers: LCCN 2021014338 (print) | LCCN 2021014339 (ebook) | ISBN 9781427141170 (hardcover) | ISBN 9781427141231 (paperback) | ISBN 9781427133465 (ebook) | ISBN 9781427134066 (epub) | ISBN 9781427141293
Subjects: LCSH: Veterinarians--Juvenile literature.
Classification: LCC SF756.28 .B46 2022 (print) | LCC SF756.28 (ebook) | DDC 636.089/069--dc23
LC record available at https://lccn.loc.gov/2021014338
LC ebook record available at https://lccn.loc.gov/2021014339